TWISTED
FAIRY TALES

The
Ninjabread
MAN

Stewart Ross

ARCTURUS

This edition published in 2020 by Arcturus Publishing Limited
26/27 Bickels Yard, 151–153 Bermondsey Street,
London SE1 3HA

Written by: Stewart Ross
Illustrated by: Chris Jevons
Designed by: Jeni Child
Edited by: Sebastian Rydberg

ISBN: 978-1-78888-493-8
CH006297NT
Supplier 13, Date 0320, Print run 10136

Printed in China

ong ago, in ancient Japan, there lived two retired ninja warriors. They no longer went on adventures but stayed happily at home and tended their garden.

"Ah!" smiled the old man. "What a good life we have!"

"Yes, indeed," replied the old woman, "Except for one thing. We have no little ninja to continue our work."

"You're right," sighed the old man. "If only we had a speedy, sneaky, and brave ninja child of our own."

The old woman thought for a moment, then said, "Husband, I have an idea!"

"We'll go up the mountain," said the old woman, "and ask Crafty Fox for his advice. He's bound to be able to help."

So, up they went to Crafty Fox's house. After giving them a cup of tea, he asked why they had come. The old woman told him how they longed for a ninja child.

"One that is speedy, sneaky, and brave," said the old man.

"Just like us," smiled the old woman.

Crafty Fox thought for a moment. "Well," he said, "I can help. Listen very carefully, and I'll tell you what to do."

The ninja couple were thrilled. At last, they would have their very own ninja child!

They were so excited that they didn't pay

much attention to Crafty Fox's instructions.

"Bake a Ninjabread Man," he explained. "Add a pinch of lemon to make him speedy, a teaspoon of ginger to make him sneaky, and just a touch of hot wasabi powder to make him brave."

"Thank you!" chorused the couple, as they hurried out of the house.

They couldn't wait to get baking.

Back home, the couple prepared the batter for a Ninjabread Man. The old man fetched a bowl, and the old woman brought a bag of rice flour.

"Right," he said, "what did Crafty Fox say we needed?"

"Lemon to make him speedy," replied the old woman.

"How much?"

The old woman scratched her head. "I don't remember exactly. A spoonful will do."

The old man squeezed a spoonful of lemon juice into the mixture.

"Now ginger to make him sneaky!" he laughed. He took a cupful of powdered ginger and threw it into the bowl.

"And wasabi powder to make him brave," said the old woman. "Make sure it's really hot!"

"It is," said the old man, taking down a jar of their most fiery wasabi. "The best!" he grinned, as he threw a handful of the green powder into the bowl and stirred it in.

When it was all mixed together, they rolled out a Ninjabread Man on the kitchen table, put him on a large tray, and popped him into the oven.

"Incredible!" gasped the old woman when she opened the oven door. "Our very own Ninjabread Man!"

"Is he alive?" asked the old man.

"Of course I'm alive!" cried the Ninjabread Man, skipping out of the oven like a deer.

"And are you speedy, sneaky, and brave?" asked the old woman.

"Aha!" he grinned, bouncing onto the kitchen table. "Just watch!"

He sprang from the table to the door, crashing through it. He kicked over a bag of rice, spilling it all over the floor. He then raised his hand and, with a leap, brought it down on the kitchen table, chopping it completely in half.

"Amazing!" smiled the old man.

The Ninjabread Man laughed. "That was nothing. Watch this!"

He grabbed a large china pot, and, with one ninja blow of his bare hands, he smashed it to pieces.

"Clever!" gasped the old woman. "But please be careful."

But the Ninjabread Man was not careful at all. Within five minutes, he had broken every pot in the house!

"Oh, dear!" groaned the old woman, as the Ninjabread Man smashed her last pot to smithereens. "This must stop!"

The little rascal grinned at her. "What must stop?"

"You must," explained the old man. "You've broken all our pots, ruined the door, spread rice all over the floor, and destroyed our kitchen table!"

The Ninjabread Man leaped into the air. "No one tells me what to do! I'm the speediest, sneakiest, and bravest ninja in the whole wide world!"

To prove it, he leaped up and hung from the ceiling lamp like a monkey!

"No more!" begged the old woman. "You've broken everything!"

The Ninjabread Man dropped to the floor as lightly as a butterfly. "Everything? Then, the speediest, sneakiest, and bravest ninja in the whole wide world will look for fun elsewhere."

With that, he jumped through the window and out into the street.

The old man took a deep breath. "Well," he sighed, "what on earth are we going to do now?"

"We must stop him before he does even more damage!" cried the old woman, hurrying out of the door. "Follow me!"

Too late!

The Ninjabread Man was already halfway down the street. Behind him, the village looked as if a whirlwind had hit it.

He had jumped onto the roof of the doctor's house and thrown down the tiles into his yard. He had then let several chickens out of their pen and knocked the farmer's apples into the gutter.

For fun, he sprang up with a wicked cry in front of a young couple out for a walk. They were so shocked that they fell backward into a muddy puddle!

The old man and old woman stared in

horror. "He's *your* Ninjabread Man!" shouted the doctor angrily. "Grab him before he causes even more trouble!"

"You're right!" replied the old woman. "We'll catch him immediately."

"We certainly will!" echoed the old man, setting off down the street. "Come here, Ninjabread Rascal! Come here!"

The old man and woman had not forgotten their own ninja skills.

"OK, old man," commanded the old woman, "you go left, and I'll go right. We'll catch the naughty ninja between us."

The old woman jumped up onto the roofs on one side of the street, and the old man did the same on the other. Roof by roof, jump by jump, they closed in on the sneaky scoundrel.

All this time, the troublesome treat stood in the middle of the street and watched. "Try, try, as hard as you can!" he laughed. "You won't catch me. I'm the Ninjabread Man!"

"Yes, we will!" shouted the old man, jumping down toward him. "Got you!"

But he hadn't. As he came down, the Ninjabread Man leaped up where the old man had been. Then, the old woman tried— and the same thing happened.

Up and down they went, more and more dizzy. At last, they crashed into each other, collapsing in a heap. "We'll never catch him on our own," panted the old man. "We need help."

The old couple made a list of their ninja friends. First was proud Master Uma, the horse.

"Please, Master Uma," they asked, "will you help us catch the naughty Ninjabread Man?"

"Of course," replied the horse. "He may be speedy, but I'm much speedier."

The old man, the old woman, and the horse then called on Mistress Ushi, the super-sneaky cow. Yes, she said, she would happily use her

16

sneakiness to help catch the Ninjabread Man.

Master Inu, the brave dog, also agreed to help. "I'm braver than any Ninjabread Man," he growled.

Finally, the five friends climbed the mountain to see Crafty Fox. "Oh, dear," he said when he heard the couple's story. "Did you add lemon, ginger, and wasabi to make a delicious Ninjabread Man, as I told you?"

"Yes," they nodded.

Crafty Fox licked his lips. "Then, I will use my craftiness to help you catch that tasty— um, naughty—Ninjabread Man," he said. "Off we go!"

"You just rest while I show you how to catch this troublesome little warrior," said Master Uma. "I'll do it without even getting my hooves dirty."

Off he trotted, and the old couple, the cow, the dog, and the fox sat on a bench to watch.

Before long, the Ninjabread Man came leaping into view. "Aha!" neighed Master Uma. "Watch me go!"

With a clatter of hooves and a splatter of dirt, he set off after the naughty ninja. Down the street they raced, between the houses and into the countryside.

Master Uma was fast, but the Ninjabread Man was faster—and nimbler. When they reached the rice farms, he jumped onto a slithery bank between two muddy fields. Master Uma tried to follow.

"Oh, no!" he cried, as he slipped off the bank. SQUELCH!

As Master Uma stood there, stuck in sticky mud, impish laughter floated over from the corner of the field: "Try, try, as hard as you can! You won't catch me. I'm the Ninjabread Man!"

"I can catch the Ninjabread Man by being sneakier than him," said Mistress Ushi.

With her spade, she dug a deep pit. Over the top, she laid twigs and leaves.

"What's that?" asked the old woman.

"It's a Ninjabread Man trap," explained Mistress Ushi proudly. "When he walks over it, the twigs will break, and he will fall into the pit."

But the sneaky ninja had been watching her. "We'll see who gets caught in that trap," he said to himself.

When Mistress Ushi was alone, the Ninjabread Man danced up and down on the edge of the pit. "Silly Mistress Cow, can't catch me now!" he chanted.

This made her so angry that she charged at him. He leaped into the air, but poor Mistress Ushi couldn't stop. Into the leaves she went and—CRASH!—down into the pit.

Leaving her in the trap, the sassy sweet danced away, singing, "Try, try, as hard as you can! You won't catch me. I'm the Ninjabread Man!"

"Master Uma and Mistress Ushi are not brave enough," growled Master Inu to the old man and woman. "I'll show you how to catch the Ninjabread Man."

He picked up his warrior stick and called out, "Hey, Ninjabread Man! Come and fight—if you're brave enough!"

The naughty ninja swung down from his hiding place in a tree by the river. "I'm speedy, and I'm sneaky," he said, "but most of all, I'm really brave. So, of course, I will fight you, Master Inu. And I will win."

He broke off a branch to make his own stick and bounced toward his opponent.

Swish! went Master Inu's stick as it missed the Ninjabread Man. Crack! went the Ninjabread Man's stick as it landed on Master Inu's head. Swish! Crack! Swish! CRA-A-ACK! Then ... SPLASH!

The Ninjabread Man had knocked Master Inu into the river!

"Try, try, as hard as you can!" laughed the naughty ninja. "You won't catch me. I'm the Ninjabread Man!"

"Don't be so sure," said a smooth voice behind the Ninjabread Man. He turned to see Crafty Fox standing there.

"You mean you're going to catch me?" chuckled the little buttery beast. "No chance!"

Crafty Fox shook his head. "Not me, dear sir. But look over there." He pointed with his paw toward the village.

Coming toward them were the old man,

the old woman, a rather muddy Master Uma, and a very angry-looking Mistress Ushi. And as the Ninjabread Man watched, they were joined by a soaked Master Inu who was now wading down the river toward him.

They were spread out in a line, so the only way that the Ninjabread Man could escape was to swim across the river.

"But I can't swim!" he wailed. "If I stay here, they'll catch me. What am I going to do?"

Crafty Fox gave him a suppertime smile and said calmly, "Don't worry, my Ninjabread friend. I have a plan. Would you like to go for a little ride?"

The Ninjabread man looked suspiciously at Crafty Fox. "A little ride?" he asked. "What do you mean?"

"What I mean," explained the Fox, "is that you hop on my tail, and I will give you a ride across the river."

"On your tail?" snorted the suspicious sweet. "Never! I don't trust you!"

"Ah, well, then I'll be going," said Crafty Fox. "Good luck!" He turned and began to walk away.

The Ninjabread Man looked at the river, and he looked at the old man, the old woman, and their three friends. They were very close now, and they were not smiling.

"Um, excuse me, Mr. Fox," called the Ninjabread Man. "Would you come back, please? I've changed my mind."

"I thought you would," nodded Crafty Fox. "There's nothing to worry about. I have always liked you. In fact, I have never seen a Ninjabread Man who is so delici … I mean, so speedy, sneaky, and brave.

"So, just jump on my tail, and off we go!"

When the old man, the old woman, Master Uma, Mistress Ushi, and Master Inu reached the riverbank, there was Crafty Fox swimming toward the other side. And on his tail, grinning happily, sat the Ninjabread Man.

"I thought you were going to catch him!" called the wife crossly.

Crafty Fox made no reply. But as the five friends watched, something strange happened.

Crafty Fox's tail started sinking into the water. "Hey!" called the Ninjabread Man. "What's going on?"

"No problem," replied Crafty Fox. "Move onto my back."

The Ninjabread Man did as he was told. Then, the back started sinking into the water.

"No problem," said Crafty Fox. "Move onto my head."

The Ninjabread Man did as he was told. Then, the head started sinking into the water.

"No problem," said Crafty Fox. "Move onto my nose."

The Ninjabread Man did as he was told, and there he sat, just above the slippery tongue and shiny white teeth of the very crafty fox.

Crafty Fox was now in the middle of the river. Sitting with his toes dangling next to the greedy jaws, the Ninjabread Man felt very uncomfortable.

"Excuse me, Mr. Fox," he began, "but do you think … Hey!"

With a twitch of his nose, Crafty Fox flicked the Ninjabread Man into the air. He opened his mouth and caught the little rascal as he came down.

SNAP! went Crafty Fox's jaws, and the Ninjabread Man disappeared.

The crowd on the bank let out a loud groan. Crafty Fox had said he would help catch the Ninjabread Man, not eat him!

For a moment, nothing happened. Then, Crafty Fox's eyes began to water. His face went from red to blue, his nose from black to scarlet. Steam hissed out of his pointed ears.

He opened his mouth and spat the Ninjabread Man high into the air like a rocket.

"H-H-HOT!" he panted. "Too much lemon! Too much spicy ginger! And way too much fiery wasabi!"

The Ninjabread Man landed on the other side of the river, and Crafty Fox swam back to his friends.

"I'm sorry," he said. "He looked delicious … But how much wasabi did you use?"

"Only a handful," said the old man.

"A handful!" exclaimed Crafty Fox. "No wonder …"

He was interrupted by a familiar voice. "Try, try, as hard as you can! You won't catch me. I'm the Ninjabread Man!"

He was right, too. The naughty ninja ran into the hills and was never seen again.